ALFIE
Alfie on Holiday

For Leah with love

Other titles in the Alfie series:

Alfie Gets in First
Alfie's Feet
Alfie Gives a Hand
An Evening at Alfie's
Alfie and the Birthday
Surprise
Alfie Wins a Prize
Alfie and the Big Boys
All About Alfie

Alfie's Christmas
Alfie Outdoors
Alfie Weather
Alfie's World
Annie Rose Is
My Little Sister
Rhymes for Annie Rose
The Big Alfie and Annie
Rose Storybook

The Big Alfie Out of
Doors Storybook
The Alfie Treasury
Alfie and Dad
Alfie and Mum
Alfie and Grandma
Alfie and His Very
Best Friend
Alfie at Nursery School

RED FOX

UK | USA | Canada | Ireland | Australia
India | New Zealand | South Africa

Red Fox is part of the Penguin Random House group of companies
whose addresses can be found at global.penguinrandomhouse.com.
www.penguin.co.uk   www.puffin.co.uk   www.ladybird.co.uk

Penguin
Random House
UK

First published 2019
001
Copyright © Shirley Hughes, 2019
The moral right of the author has been asserted

Printed in China

A CIP catalogue record for this book is available from the British Library
ISBN: 978-1-782-95878-9

All correspondence to:
Red Fox, Penguin Random House Children's, 80 Strand, London WC2R 0RL

ALFIE

Alfie on Holiday

Shirley Hughes

Red Fox

Alfie's little sister, Annie Rose, was not feeling well.
She was awake a lot in the night and kept crying.
Mum was very busy looking after her.

Dad was at work, and Alfie's best friend, Bernard, who lived nearby, was away on holiday. Alfie had no one to play with and he was very bored.

So he was very, very happy when Grandma arrived.

"Pack your bag, Alfie," she said. "I've come to take you for a few days at the seaside. Don't forget to bring your bucket and spade!"

They drove to the seaside in Grandma's car. It was a place that Alfie had never been to before. He and Grandma were going to stay at a lovely hotel with balconies that looked right out on to the beach.

As soon as they had unpacked, they held hands
and ran down across the pebbles to the big sandy beach,
where the tide was going out.

They paddled in the shallow water along the tideline.
Every time Alfie saw the sea he had forgotten how big it was,
wave after wave stretching out to meet the sky.

Next morning the sun came out, and Alfie and Grandma went for a swim. Alfie wore his armbands and clung tightly to Grandma because the water was much rougher than in the swimming pool they went to at home.

When they were dry, Grandma settled herself in a deckchair and Alfie began to build a sandcastle.

Just nearby, another boy of about Alfie's age was building a sandcastle too. His castle was bigger than Alfie's. It had a moat all around it and flags flying from the top.

After a while he said to Alfie in a friendly way: "Why don't we dig a channel between our two castles, so when the tide comes in there will be one big moat all around them?"

Together they worked very hard to make the deep connection. The tide was coming in fast now. They only just managed to finish it before the first little waves came flooding in.

Then they watched as, gradually, the two moats filled with seawater and the sides of their castles began to collapse . . .

. . . until at last Alfie's
castle was gone completely,
and only the top of the
other one was showing.
In the end, even that
was gone.

After this the boy told Alfie that his name was Lee.
His mum was sitting nearby. She and Grandma got
chatting, and they shared their picnic lunches.

That afternoon, when the tide was out, Alfie and Lee
paddled in the shallow water and collected shells and bits
of seaweed. There were lots of other children splashing
about, and Lee seemed to know most of them.

One of them had a kite, and they all
joined together to watch it fly up into the air.

"You seem to have made a friend," said Grandma as she tucked Alfie into the bed next to hers in their hotel room. Alfie went to sleep straight away, listening to the sea washing on the beach outside.

Next morning Alfie and Grandma were out on the beach early. Alfie spotted Lee and ran over to him.

But Lee seemed very busy playing catch with his friends.
Alfie tried to join in, but Lee kept throwing the ball to other people.
"Shall we go and build another sandcastle?" Alfie asked him.
But Lee did not seem to hear him.

Alfie went to sit with
Grandma. "Let's go
for a paddle," she said.

Later, when Alfie was busy digging sandcastles by himself, Lee's mum strolled by. "I'm sorry Lee hasn't had time to play with Alfie today," she said to Grandma. "He has so many friends, you see. And this afternoon he's invited to a birthday party."

So for the rest of their stay Alfie and Grandma found nice things to do together. They had ice creams,

and drew pictures in the sand,

and when the tide was out they explored rock pools and collected seaweed and shells.

When their trip was over they looked for Lee and his mum to say goodbye. But they were nowhere to be seen. "Perhaps he's gone to another birthday party," said Grandma.

They arrived home to find Mum and Dad and Annie Rose on the doorstep to greet them.

Annie Rose was much better, and she was so pleased to see Alfie again that she hugged him round the waist.

"By the way, Bernard has come home from his holiday," said Mum.
"He and his mum are coming to tea this afternoon."

When Bernard arrived, he was so pleased to see Alfie again that he
wrestled him to the floor and they rolled over and over.

Then they went into the back garden and sat in the Alfie and Bernard clubhouse, which was in the bush in Alfie's back garden; the one that nobody was allowed into unless they were invited, because it was only for truly special friends.